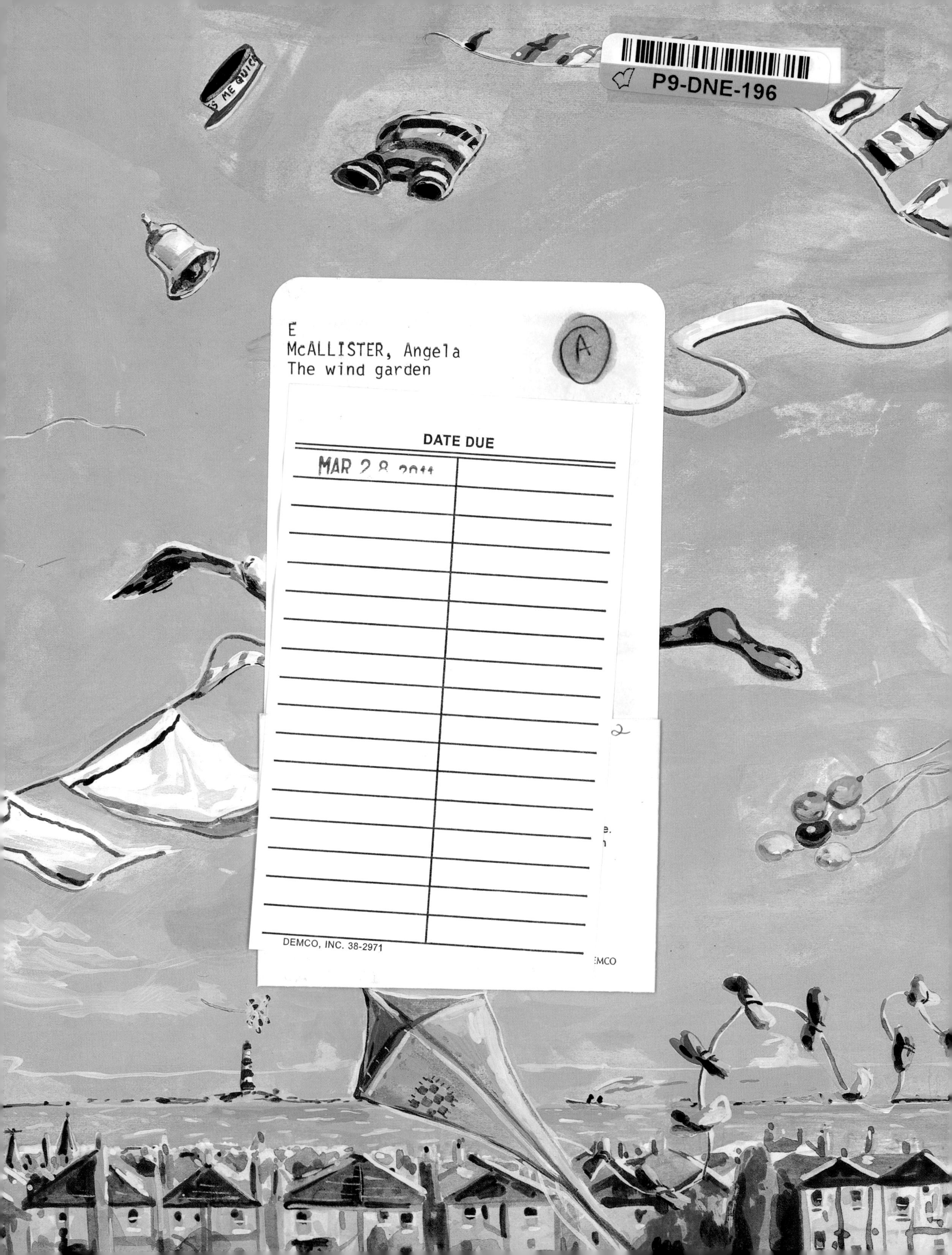

For Antje with love – AM
For Benjamin and his parents – CF

Text copyright © 1994 by Angela McAllister
Illustrations copyright © 1994 by Claire Fletcher
First published in Great Britain by The Bodley Head, Ltd.
All rights reserved. No part of this book may be reproduced or utilized in any form or by any
means, electronic or mechanical, including photocopying and recording, or by any information
storage and retrieval system, without permission in writing from the Publisher. Inquiries should
be addressed to Lothrop, Lee & Shepard Books,
a division of William Morrow & Company, Inc., 1350 Avenue of the Americas,
New York, New York 10019.
Printed in Singapore
First U.S. Edition 1995   1   2   3   4   5   6   7   8   9   10
Library of Congress Cataloging in Publication Data
McAllister, Angela. The wind garden / by Angela McAllister; illustrated by Claire Fletcher.
p.   cm.   Summary: On his rooftop, Ellie's grandfather needs a special kind of garden that
the wind won't destroy. ISBN 0-688-13280-4 [1. Winds—Fiction.   2. Grandfathers—Fiction.]
I. Fletcher, Claire, ill.   II. Title. PZ7.W47825Wi   1994 [E]—dc20   93-37435 CIP AC

The Wind Garden

Angela McAllister & Claire Fletcher

LOTHROP, LEE & SHEPARD BOOKS   NEW YORK

Grandpa lived at the top of a high house. His old legs wouldn't take him up and down the long staircase anymore, so he stayed at home. Ellie came to visit every day.

"I miss the park, Ellie," said Grandpa. "I miss walking in the gardens."

So Ellie brought some seeds and flowerpots. Together they planted the seeds, put them out on Grandpa's roof, and waited.

The seeds sprouted. They grew thin little stems and tiny leaves. But out on the roof, the wind was always blowing. The seedlings couldn't grow in the wind, and they died.

"That bad old wind," said Ellie. "Where does it come from, Grandpa?"

"No one can guess," said Grandpa, "nobody knows, where the wind comes from, where the wind goes."

Ellie wanted a garden for Grandpa. She brought him some strong sunflowers. Together they put them out on the roof and watered each one. The flowers grew up and up toward the sun.

But out on the roof, the wind was always blowing. It rocked the sunflowers harder and harder until their tall stems broke.

"That wicked old wind," said Ellie. "Where is it blowing to, Grandpa?"

"No one can guess, nobody knows, where the wind comes from, where the wind goes," said Grandpa. "I think that old wind is just trying to tell me I live too high in the sky for a garden."

That night Ellie stayed at Grandpa's house. In bed she could hear the wind. With a strong blow, it pushed the window open. Ellie climbed out onto the roof.

The wind danced around her. Round and round it rushed, until Ellie was dancing, too. Then, with a great gust, the wind lifted Ellie up off Grandpa's roof and into the starry sky.

"I'm going to where the wind blows!" Ellie laughed, and she wished Grandpa were flying, too.

Soon she came to a little wood on a mountaintop. The wind gently set her down. Everywhere the trees were hung with things the wind had carried away: kites and balloons, hats and handkerchiefs, colored flags, church bells, and lost laundry.

It was the wind's garden.

The wind blew proudly. It made everything
flutter and dance. It made everything rustle and
chime, swinging, spinning, shimmering in the
sun. Ellie whirled among the trees. If only
Grandpa could see the wind garden.

Ellie saw a kite she had lost long ago. As she took its tail, the wind lifted her up and carried her back to Grandpa's house.

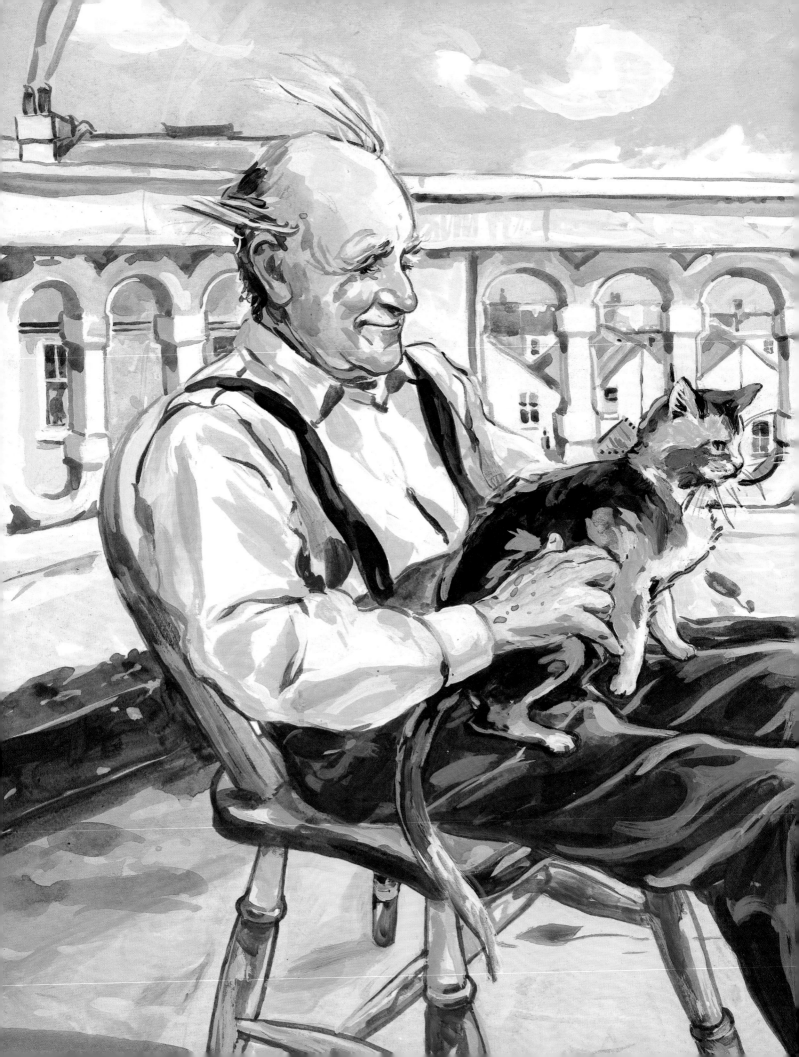

The next day Grandpa sat, remembering, on his empty roof.

Ellie brought out a box. Together they pulled out flags and chimes, whirligigs, windmills, and bells.

"Here is your garden, Grandpa," she said. "Here is a garden to share with the wind."

Out on the roof, the wind was always blowing. It made
everything swing, spin, and shimmer in the sun.
  Grandpa smiled. "No one can guess, nobody knows,
where the wind comes from, where the wind goes."

But somebody knew.
Ellie knew where the wind blew,
but she wasn't going to tell.